In These Days of Dancing

B. A. PAUL

For Ranveig.
There's this tale of different endings, a pond full of of swans, and a goose
in a wig that must figure out how to market this thing because you kept me
grounded...

Contents

I Heard There'll Be Swans

My Dearest Sister,

With trembling hand, I pen you this in the darkest and brightest of hours with a heart that is one moment trilling with love and light and the next near crushed to the depths of the earth.

The quill shakes with each stroke, fear and excitement intermingled.

The dichotomy of all emotion...

Yes, Lily. I can hear you now. "Stop being so flowery and poetic. You are not a poet, Reniah."

To which I will give my trusted, curt reply: "One can make an attempt, can't one?"

I suppose I've waxed flowery because I don't know what to feel, much like that day when we stole old Annie's mop and pretended it was a horse, galloping through the halls—giddy one moment, guilt-ridden the next.

No matter what wave of emotion I'm engulfed in, I believe I know what *you* will feel tomorrow when you read this letter. I try not to dwell on the tears I cannot wipe from your flushed cheeks, nor on the way your bottom lip will quiver, nor on the way you'll square your shoulders to regain your composure, only to lose it again when no one is looking.

I know you well, my beloved sister, and I am so, so sorry.

But regardless of the timing and tumultuousness the following days will no doubt bring, your heart was destined to break once you learned of my condition. I hope reading this will perhaps offer a tiny bit of hope to reassemble the cracked pieces—like that day we used molasses to mend old Annie's vase. A little lopsided, but it worked rather well. Remember how red Annie's face got when she'd seen what we did? How sticky our hands and dresses were? Mother was furious...

Brooms and vases. I'm waxing nostalgic. I'll get on with it then...

Lily, I did exactly what you told me not to do, but the fault doesn't lie with you. Yes, Mother tasked you with looking after me, but we both know that no one has ever successfully directed my comings and goings. (Though many have made attempts, haven't they?)

That is, until now.

And ever since I met the Dowager of Bristol, my fate was sealed.

Yes, I met with her this very day. Yes, you warned me of the rumors and of the Dowager's reputation.

But, you see, sister, I am—I was—desperate.

Desperate enough to meet with the rumored witch...

I adjust in the bed, precariously balancing the inkwell and stationery on my lap. Mother would be aghast at my posture and the fact that I've already dripped ink onto my shift. And the bedclothes.

No matter.

I close my eyes, memories swirl like the ink in the well. And heaven curse those days of desperation, but at least they spurred me to relentlessly pursue an ending of my choice rather than allow this dreadful illness to rob me of my life *and* my estate.

Not that the latter matters much in the end, not to me anyway. But I won't tell my sister this. She's the one who must sojourn on in this relentless world of courtship and seasons and expectations...

I dab at the bedclothes. These blotches won't even be a bother to poor, pitiful Phoebe. She'll be too busy committing a crime on my behalf to worry with stained linens.

Funny. How the most important elements of daily living—spotless textiles, impeccably decorated desserts, and table settings measured to the centimeter—become laughably trivial.

Death will do that.

I lean my head against the headboard. Another wave of nausea courses through me. Every fiber of my being feels it these days. For months now. It'll pass, but not before it takes another pint of my energy —and today took ten pints. The trip into town. The walk to the Dowager. The trip back here to collapse into bed after Phoebe helped me back into my nightclothes.

My lungs fill as I slowly breathe in, the hint of wisteria tickling my nostrils. Phoebe wanted to change out the vase with roses. But for my final days in my childhood bedroom, I longed to bathe in the purple essence that adorns every nook and cranny of Shedd House.

Besides, there'll be roses aplenty tonight...

I resituate the writing on my lap and dip the nib again.

Oh, my Dear One...

Do you remember the day at the pond over in Kirworth? That spring? We'd snuck away from Nanny and dodged Annie and stole the ribbons from the maypoles. We acted more like little boys than little girls as we tied the silks to the ends of oak sticks. We'd fought over the red ribbon. I gave in and let you have it. I took the yellow one. The things you remember...

Then we tied rocks to the other ends of the ribbons.

How mad Mother was over her precious ribbons.

How despondent we were that fish don't eat rocks.

Oh, but the swans! Do you remember them, Lily? How they gathered at the far end of the pond once Nanny and Mother confiscated our fishing poles and halted the flying rocks?

Those elegant white feathers and graceful gliding strides over the water? There must've been a dozen pairs of them along the water's edge. When they'd swim toward one another, for a brief second, their curved necks made the shape of a heart, the water rippling from behind them...

Maybe you were too little to notice that detail. But I wasn't.

I became obsessed with swans. Well, you know this. I drove Mother nearly mad when I was learning my needlework, embroidering—or attempting to embroider—the elegant birds on pillowcases and hand-kerchiefs. I'm smiling now as I think of how she declared, "Reniah, no one wants to blow their noses on bird beaks."

I learned all I could about the swans. Their courtship is glorious—and they're far better dancers than half the gentlemen scribbling their names on my dance card during my season...

And they mate for life.

Even at that tender young age, I started to dream. To be paired with someone forever. A never-ending dance with the one who would complete my heart.

And none of the gents on my dance card ever fit the bill...

⁓

These are all the words I can muster for the moment. Another wave of ill rolls over me.

I allow my head to rest again as the nausea does its evil thing. What would I do without Phoebe?

Rot in this bed, alone. That's what. Phoebe got me to the Dowager none too soon.

Outside my window, the sun has reached its peak. My attire for the evening hangs on the wardrobe's ajar door, blowing slightly with the spring breeze. The red ribbons and pearl combs await Phoebe's magic touch on the dressing table. She'll tame my mane, help me dress, and call for the carriage, and then...

I let the thought go—I need to focus on Lily and easing her mind and heart as best I can. I dip my quill into the inkwell, trying not to dribble any more black all over the white spread—though I'm not sure it can be helped with my shaking hands...

⁓

Oh, Lily. That's what finding love has been for me: fishing with ribbons and rocks. Season after season. Me! *The* Reniah Shedd! I cringe at the shame I brought to our estate when, even after the blessing of the Queen, I'd not been picked—or rather was too picky—that first go-round.

And the second and the third...

I remember our conversation about matchmakers. There'd been several such women spring up over the years. I thought perhaps one of them could find me my swan. You warned me about the Dowager of Bristol, so naturally, being the belligerent soul that I am, the Dowager of Bristol is exactly who I fixated on.

One must make an attempt when death is chasing one down.

In the throes of this illness, I found myself on the Dowager's stoop.

From the great beyond, I can see you cringe, Lily. I can see you draw the curtains while you read this, seated at your writing desk as if eyes from outside would spy and declare my business through the country-side, bringing more disgrace to our family.

But I needed help.

And help the Dowager did. She also gave a whopping dollop of hope as sweet as molasses—and much stickier.

There was even a sign, Lily!

Swans! I couldn't believe my eyes. I didn't believe them at first, thinking the weakness was causing my vision to play tricks with my mind. Then I fought off a tickle of fear that rose up. What if the Dowager's magic might be seeping from under the door and had me in a spell even before speaking with the woman?

But neither of those were the case.

Lily! There was a pair of swans engraved around the door knocker, their necks entwined in a permanent heart. This was it, Lily. If ever there was a sign, or a dab of magic, or a hallucination—no matter. I knew this was it! No more fishing with rocks!

The Dowager sent word: His name is Breck Rampkin.

And, yes, I know his brother has a reputation for being an—

Oooo! Sorry for the ink smudge. I'm writing this from bed. I so wish I could fight with you in person about this, but... not today.

Today, my dearest Lily, I shall be wed to Lord Breck Rampkin.

It's not how I dreamed it would go at all.

There will be no courtship or need for chaperones. You'll have to get past this.

There will be no reading of the banns. I suppose you'll get over that, given your disdain for that practice to begin with.

There will be no grand preparations. I know you were looking forward to overseeing Phoebe and the housemaids if I ever did settle for a name on my dance card. I suppose you'll eventually forgive me.

There will be no public ceremony to witness the union (though there will be witnesses—the Dowager has promised it's all a legitimate union so long as the paperwork leaves out the mention of magic, that is).

And, Lily! I heard there'll be swans!

I'm truly at peace with all this.

What breaks me in two is that you will not be next to me. Carrying the train of my dress. Holding my bouquet of roses and wisteria as rings are exchanged. Blushing during the wedded kiss. The dancing and feasting. Hanging my head out of the carriage to watch you wave us goodbye as I start a new life with my husband. I'd planned on watching you until you were too small to see even though I know you'd likely stand in the drive, filled to the brim with pride and joy, long after the carriage disappeared.

These things, Lily, are what eat at me. I swear this pain is worse than what the illness hands me on the regular.

Remember that other day at the Kirworth? When we stole the white table runners from the prep area? Poor, poor Annie—I think this is the day she gave up trying to reign us in. And goodness! I just realized we were little thieves, Lily. Brooms and ribbons and table runners. Molasses from the pantry! Thieves!

We were always up to something, weren't we?

Remember how we grabbed handfuls of wildflowers from the tables and made crowns fit for princesses and braided our hair? We draped ourselves in those white runners and took turns parading as brides through the garden maze. And the topiaries? Those were our witnesses and—and our betrothed. If memory serves, I married a giraffe that day and you were wedded to a boxwood bear.

Hold on to that memory, Lily. All of them. Write them down and remember. I'll always be with you in those memories of childhood and girlhood.

As I go to meet my Breck this evening, I'll imagine you are there with me. If I imagine hard enough... perhaps, by some turn of magic or of time falling in on itself, you might be.

I know this stings. Phoebe has held me many times in the last few days as sobs shook my body over this.

But my directions from the Dowager are very clear. If I am to keep my loved ones safe, I mustn't include them. It guts me that I even need Phoebe's help—but I've got a feeling she'll make it okay.

And I do so want to keep you safe. If you came, and things fall apart after I depart, you'd be culpable. Conspiring with witches and magic and such.

So take heart, dear—

~

A fit of coughing interrupts my ink flow. I watch as the wet ink glistens on the last few words I penned before it sinks into the paper. I'm not sure how long I sit here, watching the ink dry. I hope Lily will do what I've asked. I hope she starts writing things down. Memories. Stories. I'll live on in this world, even as I'm whisked to the next. She'll be okay. I know she will...

The breeze floats through the room, sending an excited shiver of gooseflesh up my arms. I know I need to conserve energy, and this letter is taking it out of me, but it's my Lily. And since she won't be with me, I have to give her this...

Deep breath.

Dip the pen.

Begin again...

~

My union with Lord Breck Rampkin will solve our—your—estate problems. Once the Dowager brings around the Marquess, that is. I've no doubt she'll succeed in this effort. Despite Marquess Rampkin's ruthlessness, his estate is well in order and my union with Breck—marriage! Can you believe it?—is to be tonight.

I'm marrying because I happened to do exactly what you told me not to do and I went to town with my lady's maid and found the witch. But don't blame her for that—Phoebe or the witch. They're not at fault for their lot in life no more than you or I are at fault for my illness.

The Dowager has promised us a gorgeous ceremony, though it will be with limited witnesses, and her brother, the vicar, will ensure all things are legal.

Lord Breck is not ill of body, but he's ill to his soul with loneliness and despises the estate business. He's a kind soul, according to the Dowager, one who's willing to make such a sacrifice to not be alone in the end—his end will be mine. Mine his. He's willing to take my hands and dance with me. And we'll be together and not lonely. Joined forever.

It's the price of love.

Loving deeply, hurting deeply, losing deeply.

But eternity is deep and wide and a whole world of possibility awaits on the underside of the pond.

For the here and now, dear Lily, I have a few requests. To which I know a ball of rage has welled up in your ribcage because who am I, after causing all this pain and chaos, to request anything?

But one can make an attempt, can't one?

If you're reading this letter in the drawing room, no doubt you're aware of the missing portrait. Don't blame sweet Phoebe. She only did what she was told. I'm not sure what will become of the portrait, but I am quite sure after the witch is through, there's a good chance nothing will be recovered of it.

Take heart, Lily, because I wasn't fond of the portrait to begin with. When I sat for it, I was in the beginnings of my illness. That pink in my cheeks wasn't the stroke of the artist's brush— I'd been flush with fever. Oooh! And that artist! He was our dear mother's pretentious pick, but I didn't care for him, which made matters worse, sitting there so still and so ill. He was—well.

Promise me this, Lily, if your dance card remains lackluster, for the love of all that's good and holy, don't panic and pick the painter. Find the Dowager or any number of other witches for their matchmaking prowess before you pick the painter.

Replace the missing portrait with the previous one. The one from before I was sick. The one from before. Remember me from when life had hope and purpose. Because, dear Sister, it does now.

❁

The door to my bedroom opens. Phoebe enters with a smile and a small tray of scones. She places a bouquet gently on my nightside table. Though I don't know if I'll be carrying the flowers during the ceremony, I'd planned on carrying some from the house to the carriage this evening. To pretend. Pretend that Lily is with me, fussing each of the petals into perfect positions.

"Thank you." My voice cracks.

"Don't speak. Save your energy. Finish your letter and I'll see that Lily gets it."

I nod. What would I do without Phoebe?

She sets the tray next to me on the bed. I have no appetite. Eating is a struggle. But strawberry scones are my favorite, and I'll give them a try when I can bring myself to write "Love, Reniah."

Phoebe notices the splotches on the bedclothes, but she doesn't comment on them. I must've dozed off at some point, given the extra ink stains.

I know it's time to wrap up this message to Lily. I think I'm dawdling. No, I know I am. If I keep writing, I won't have to say goodbye for real. I really am at peace and in torment all at the same time.

A dichotomy of emotions.

As I wipe tears I decide I cannot wait to finish the letter before having a taste, I reach for a scone and take the tiniest bite. A burst of strawberry jam brings more tears to my eyes—will the hereafter have strawberry jam? Out of sheer will I force the scone down. I need some strength for what's to come and an empty stomach isn't the correct approach.

I eat another tiny treat and examine the flowers in my bouquet. Tiny roses. A couple of sprigs of wisteria, and—Oh! Bless Phoebe's heart!

~

Dear Sister, I must hurry now, so forgive the messy scroll. My strength is fading, the sun will dip soon, and my beloved awaits me.

To finish up my requests, don't blame the footman, either. He is to Lord Breck as Phoebe is to me—a trusted confidant and a brave, kind soul.

And as I said before, write things down. Remember. Visit those times of long ago often—I live there with you. Most of all, live the days without guilt or fault, for there are neither of those in you regarding me.

I can feel you tensing up, Lily. I imagine your face is red by now. Your fists balled. So take a deep breath for me—we're almost to the end.

Since you cannot be with me this evening, I will tell you what the Dowager said of the ceremony—at least the parts I'm allowed to speak of.

I'll wear a most magnificent gown, Lily. More gorgeous than the one for my debutante ball. Really! Scarlet layers and pearl bodice. And it shimmers in just the right light... Every little girl's dream. My hair will be done up in braids with pearls and ribbons (it's my turn for the red one).

Grasping my bouquet to my chest, I'll slide into the carriage and meet Breck at the Rampkin's pond. The vicar will perform the ceremony, and the Dowager, well, for all we know, she's just a witness, along with my lady's maid and Breck's footman.

Then I'll dance. Dance! In his arms and around and over the pond, I'll dance. I can barely walk right now, but the witch promised— I'll be able to dance!

The whole time I'll cling to Breck with one hand, and in the other, I'll cling to my bouquet of red roses, purple wisteria—and a single white lily. (I swear this lily glimmers as if it itself is enchanted...)

So you'll be there with me even though you can't be.

And he and I will be one and whole. No more pain. No more sorrow. Pure, intense joy and love forevermore.

And Lily?

I heard there'll be swans...

Love, Reniah

Truth Be Told

Eldon Parish Clergy Ledger
26 April 1818
Come this day to be wed:
Lady Raniah Shedd of Bristol and Lord Breck Rampkin of Eldon.
Reading of the banns waived due to special circumstances.
Stood in witness:
Phoebe Bartlett of Bristol and Phillip Godwin of Eldon
Performed and Signed:
William Lockridge, Eldon Parish Vicar

Grimoire of William Lockridge, The Now and Again Warlock of Eldon

Reading of the banns waived. Of course they are! Make my life harder. Bring my record keeping under scrutiny. I genuinely embrace the era I'm in, whatever era that may be. And the Church of this era does adore all things immaculate.

My sister likes to make things complicated. Test my wits and try my patience.

I know I do whine, but this will be the longest day in this era. In five of these eras. The haste! The commotion! She's sent word she's used two colors this time. Two! The last time that happened was in another century on another continent. Fourteen couples fell in love, and war broke out.

I can't live through another war. I do hope she's honed her skills.

This is unfortunate timing. I've become attached to this place. The rush of weddings. The births nine months later—give or take a few weeks here or there. Of course, I've had to bury a few, but that comes with the territory. Little Marcell is particularly fond of the baptisms, taking a refreshing dip in the font, no one being the wiser.

The holy water does him a world of good, truth be told.

I look up from my writing, ledgers and record books lay open on my desk, ready for my keen review of my time here as vicar. I'll add a parenthetical notation for the incumbent to provide the most clarity possible for this holy changing of the guard. These books will be left.

The tome I'm filling now will come with me. My personal grimoire for spells and to detail the comings and goings of my witch of a sister so as I may keep some semblance of sanity as we hop to and fro about the eons.

"I've so much paperwork, Marcell!" I feel him skitter under my vestments, a little wiggle here. A flick of an ear there. The faint aroma of stale cheese...

The incumbent vicar will be pleased with the order of things. I take pride in my work.

But so much paperwork. And now bonus paperwork in the likely case of a bonus ceremony. Maddening. My sister drives me mad!

"*One*, Marcell. Just one bonus is what I told my sister I could manage on such a last minute's notice with the Church of England about to do an audit."

My black quill, a gift from my sister the witch, stands ready. I could wave my own spells over the pages of ledgers and record books, making my life easier, but I do take pride in doing human things as humanly as possible.

Two colors. Double vials.

I rub my temples. What I'd love to do now is to loosen my bands, kick back with a quarter-keg of Kirschwasser, toss Marcell a little brioche and stilton, and take a doze, truth be told.

Instead, I dip my nib and begin again.

Letters Not Sent

My Dear Margie,

You'll want to burn this letter (for both our sakes) and pretend you never got it. As for the others, do with them as you see fit once you see how events transpire. Perhaps you'll burn them, too.

Perhaps you'll send them.

Perhaps you'll start a gossip column to rival Lady Gwen's.

But you must burn this one. As sure as I've burned the breakfast scones.

I cannot begin to express what's happened in the last few hours. The grieving. The mayhem. The thievery. Thievery! I'm going to jail.

Or to the stocks.

I cannot for the life of me tell you how much I'll miss you. Please look after Posset lest she get her whiskers in a knot. Though most of my time is spent with Lady Reniah, Posset is accustomed to routine...

Would you listen to me? Rambling on about a silly cat when I'm going to jail. I know it.

Two months ago, being on the shelf was my biggest source of agony —a life devoted to servitude. Though the Shedds are overall kind and I could see myself with this household until I had wrinkles as deep as the chef's, you know my heart, Margie. You and I often talk of longing for companionship beyond the other handmaids, and—I'm getting ahead of myself.

I can hear you say, "Stop beating around the bush, Phoebe, just say what you intend."

Here it is: I've conspired with a witch—at least, I think she's a witch. After all she's put us through, she'd better be a witch. Me and Lady Reniah and Lord Breck Rampkin and his footman, and—

I need to back up. I'm so scattered and I've burned my lady's scones. I'm writing to you in haste between so many tasks and all while trying to keep my letter-writing out of sight of the chef and the rest of Shedd House kitchen staff—God love them every one, but they're so nosy, as staff often are.

That's what got me in trouble, Margie. What started it all. Being nosy.

I'm nothing more than a cliché of a lady's maid. I often wonder what would've become of me and Lady Reniah had I not stumbled upon her unsent letters. Maybe the same fate, but with less guilt? I'm so guilty, Margie. I just had to get it out.

But I *did* stumble upon those letters, and I *did* untie the red ribbon binding the pile, and I *did*, as ashamed as I am to admit it, read them.

Every last one of them.

Oh, goodness. Telling on myself like this. I'm a nervous wreck. A nervous, nosy wreck. Even worse than that batch of ninnies over at Kirworth Mansion. You know the scandal they caused when—

I pause my quill mid-air.

No, no, no, Phoebe. You mustn't veer off. Time is wasting.

Ooh. This would be so much easier in person. I could spill all my secrets to Margie and hand her my little calico kitty for safekeeping, but there's no time.

I blot out that last sentence. The last two sentences. This letter will be a positive mess of ink and smudge, but it'll have to do. It matches my mind's madness.

The chef is coming around from the pantry; I've tuned my ears to the thuds of his shoes. I throw a dishtowel over the inkwell and stuff the letter—ink blotches not dry—into my apron. By the end of the day, I suppose it won't matter what happens to my apron.

The chef examines me up and down. I'm covered in flour. His eyes land on my sleeve, where a dollop of strawberry jam lingers. The jam turned out nicely, but, seeing as how I burned the scones, I've nothing to put the jam on.

I square my shoulders and muster my best smile. "I'll be out of your kitchen soon enough. I want to cheer up my lady with her favorite—"

"I don't care. Be done and be gone before dinner." The chef eyes me up and down again and disappears down the hallway.

"Yes, sir," I call after him as I pull the letter from my apron pocket and uncover the inkwell. What a mess I've made.

I must focus fast, Margie. In between all my tasks today. The scones, the bouquet, the packing of my belongings. I'd tell you where I plan to go after tonight, if I only knew, but I don't know. And even if I did, I'd never come to you and put you in such a predicament.

I need to start from the beginning.

I was about my duties, tending to my lady, and though I'd thought she'd not been in the pink of late, she swore to me she was fine. She was under the pressure of another season and finding a suitable match and the affairs of the estate. I tried to mind my business.

Well, no Margie. I don't mind my business, do I?

I mind Lady Reniah's business.

So when I came across the letters—she'd been spending so much time at her writing desk, sending me to market for ink and ink alone —I had to take a glance. They weren't sealed, you see, nor were they in envelopes, just doubled neatly. It was so easy to slip off the ribbon and use one finger to unfold the page. To pick up on words here or there.

And, oh, my heart, Margie. Lady Reniah was carrying—is carrying —such a burden. All on her own. From the first few lines on that first page, I found myself overtaken. I slipped into my lady's chair and had undone all the letters. Not just with one finger either—both hands! And I cried so many tears.

The letters were addressed to her sister, Lady Lily, and several to her aunts.

Lady Reniah wrote of the agony when she learned of her illness. She wrote of sparing the family the same dark days that surrounded their mother's death. She wrote of me—and that broke my heart. How she trusted me and was about to tell me this secret because, soon, she'd be too ill to tend to her own welfare.

She scolded her sister and aunts for being so tossed about with what would become of Shedd House should Reniah or Lily not wed a man with an appropriate title, so much so that none of them even noticed Reniah slipping out of this obligation or that. Leaving events early under one guise or another. Dodging this gentleman caller or that one.

My lady despised all the gentlemen callers—all wanting the prestige of marrying the daughter of the Dutchess but none capable of carrying an intellectual conversation past business affairs.

Or dreaming. Lady Reniah wanted someone to dream with...

Oh, Margie, I am ashamed of myself for reading the letters. So personal. So...

And I was beyond mortified when I looked up to find Lady Reniah in the doorway, leaning on the frame, pale as a ghost, watching me read her secrets.

I jot one sentence after another in the middle of mixing another batch of scones. Lady Reniah has no appetite, but she'll need something on her stomach before we leave for Rampkin Castle. The first batch was meant for lunch—this batch will have to wait for evening, because I've got business to tend to in the garden.

And in my quarters, packing to leave life as I know it.

And in Reniah's quarters, laying out her attire for the evening.

But first the garden. I screw the lid on the inkwell, stuff the letter and quill and well into my pocket. I dust my hands on my apron, a lot of good that did them, and head to the back garden, wondering if I should tell Margie of this part. She'll know I've conspired with the Dowager of Bristol on behalf of Lady Reniah, but does she need to know I went back a second time?

I can't think of myself right now.

I reach the spot in the garden where the lilies bloom—or where they will bloom given a few more weeks, but we don't have weeks.

We have just this day.

The sun is bright and the breeze refreshing. This is my favorite spot on the whole of the Shedd estate and the bench is so inviting. I pick the single blossom that was not there a few hours ago, amazed at how white and bright it is, and I must sit and gather myself. I pull out my writing from my apron and try to stay on topic.

After the shock of finding me with her letters in hand, and on my lap, and scattered on the floor at my feet, in typical Reniah Shedd style, my lady stuck up her bosoms and lifted her chin. "I suppose the cat's out of the bag, yes?"

I apologized all over myself as I gathered up the letters. She said no need, that I'd find out most of that news soon enough.

And though I adore her for forgiving me such a violation, I loathed lugging the weight of my guilt and this secret.

So many visits to the doctor, whom Reniah also swore to secrecy lest she broadcast his infidelities at the next grand ball. He didn't say a word, but his eyes widened and his chin quivered enough for me to believe the doctor was bound by duty and honor to keep quiet.

His black bag became a thing of my nightmares, but my lady didn't seem phased at all the poking and prodding and medicines.

On more than one occasion, I begged Reniah to tell her family so she could have more support. But she wouldn't hear of it. "In time, Phoebe, and now's not the time." Over and over.

She confided in me, Margie. What was I to do? Reniah was set on sparing her kin what they went through with Dutchess Shedd. That the same illness should take both mother and daughter guts me. I wonder what will become of Lily...

Oooh. I can't think of that. My loyalty is to Reniah, and I can't think of that...

So we kept it hidden amid all the pressure my lady was under to find a suitable match. The whole time knowing she'd not make a suitable wife for anyone—be he a buffoon or gallant prince. For as soon as she was wed, even if she'd live to see the ceremony, she'd be in the throes of her illness and be gone.

But the pressure of society and Lily and the aunts? What will become of the Shedd Estate?

That's what did it, Margie. This morning she told me to pack her day bag and call for the carriage. We were going to meet the Dowager of Bristol.

"But I heard she's a witch, my lady."

"Exactly the kind of help I need, Phoebe."

Who am I to argue with a dying woman?

I did as I was told. It was the least I could do after violating my lady's privacy by reading those letters.

We had the driver drop us blocks away, which was so taxing on Lady Reniah. I wondered if she'd be able to walk that far, let alone back again. But when Reniah puts her head to something, there's no stopping her.

The walk seemed to invigorate her, at least for a moment. The color returned. She looked no worse for the wear, and possibly better than I'd seen her in weeks, after that stint.

I stayed at her elbow as we climbed the Dowager's stoop, worried the whole time we'd be spotted—Lady Reniah Shedd, blessed by the Queen during her debutante season, at a matchmaker's door would be bad enough. Let alone a rumored witch. But the Dowager, witch or not, seemed to believe she could help my lady with her problems—the estate problem and the love problem.

I don't know what will happen tonight. I don't know what will happen the next day. Will I be free? Will the footman be free? If we're free, we're running, Margie.

Will we be caught and hanged by sunrise?

Left on the gibbets for days?

Will the Dowager make good on all the hype? Rumor has it that the

Magical Dowager of Bristol is a fraud and should be hanged. I'll hang her myself if she hurts my lady.

But I don't think she will, and I'll tell you why because you'll be burning this letter, right?

I believe her to be a real witch. You see, my lady grieves that her sister will not be present for this wedding. I wanted to put a lily in with the roses as a surprise, but Shedd House lilies are not in bloom yet. So I returned to the Dowager for the second time in a day, this very day, looking over my shoulder and trembling the whole way. I explained my lady's predicament. The Dowager asked me to make up a parcel with a bit of stilton the size of a thimble and a bite—just a single bite—of brioche.

All I could figure were these were items for a spell, so I didn't ask questions; the less I know, the better (I am learning my nosy little lessons). The ingredients are in Shedd House pantry, so I told the Dowager I would do so. She smiled and handed me the tiniest glass bottle of blue liquid. She told me to dab it on the green of the plant as soon as I returned to Shedd House. That I'd have what I desired right on time.

Margie, it bloomed! Just the one, but it's the whitest, brightest blossom I've ever seen. It almost—glows. Just perfect to tuck into Reni-ah's bouquet. A lily for Lily.

So I believe her to be a real witch. And I believe her to be a kind soul because who would oblige a request so simple as a single flower if one were evil?

I must tend to my lady now. She's been writing all day, too, between fits of illness and exhaustion. I suppose I'm lucky this letter was penned between fits of baking and flower-picking.

I'll make sure my lady has eaten a scone or two. Dress her. Plait her hair with ribbons and pearls. Lady Reniah has embroidered Lady Lily a handkerchief—one with swans to be left with the letter. I'll lay a sprig of wisteria on the davenport for Lady Lily to find upon her return tomorrow.

I suppose this is my way of softening the blow. I can't imagine Lady Lily's reaction when she reads what's become of her sister.

I can't imagine your reaction when you read what I've been up to all these days.

Feed Posset for me. A few scraps of chicken from the buffet a couple of times a week. He'll miss the scraps I've gleaned from My Lady's uneaten leftovers, and I do feel awful about taking food from the ill.

Uneaten food.

Unsent letters.

What a shameful mess I am. I hope my last acts this evening, if they are to be my last ones, make up for the wrong I've done.

Yours truly,

Phoebe

P.S. I write these last words in utter haste—this is the longest letter I've ever written and with all the bobbling of the inkwell through my many tasks today, I'm almost out of ink, but I need to tell this to someone, Margie.

Though I've only caught sight of him a time or two, Lord Rampkin's footman is a thing of beauty.

There. I said it.

Yes, he's a man but he's a beautiful one. Since I want with my whole heart to be someone's forever—it might as well be him. A man that would risk his life and freedom for another? Gallant as any Earl or Duke at any ball I've watched from the sidelines.

If I survive this night, I shall offer my wish to the Dowager. I've aided my lady in all ways possible and made up the parcel of cheese and bread the Dowager requested, so she knows I'll make good on anything she might ask of me. I have no portrait of my own and no one to steal it for me if I did, but perhaps she's got another method to join two hearts, though I've no idea how the footman would feel about this.

If I had more time, I suppose I'd write him a letter and ask.

But I've no time and not much ink.

And if I had the time and the ink, my better judgment would kick in, stifling this silly dream from a silly lady's maid.

Oh, Margie. I suppose if I did write a letter, I'd fold the letter in half and stuff it under my mattress. Leave it unsent.

My Right Big Toe

Eldon Parish Clergy Ledger
26 April 1818
Come this day to be wed:
Lady Raniah Shedd of Bristol and Lord Breck Rampkin of Eldon.
Reading of the banns waived due to special circumstances.
Stood in witness:
Phoebe Bartlett of Bristol and Phillip Godwin of Eldon
Performed and Signed:
William Lockridge, Eldon Parish Vicar

Grimoire of William Lockridge, The Now and Again Warlock of Eldon

I swear, my sister the witch could turn any holy man into a drunkard. She claims me to be daft, but she's the reason I lose mental capacity by the week.

I fear my memory will at some point fade. I fear I'll forget to remember what a witch my sister really is. This is why I write all these events in my grimoire. Oh, of course, I write down spells that work, and spells that don't.

Mine work, hers don't—or they have such far-reaching consequences that I've forbid her to use a few of those bloody bottles ever again. I should remember to check on the Pharaoh's family—next time we're through that way and era. I'd bet my right big toe they've not recovered.

And it is *right* big toe. That's what Mother always said. But my sister the witch claims to have a perfect memory and declares Mother's saying was "I'd bet my left big toe."

Writing here for the record: It's the right one.

My sister should know this given the fact that Mother's right big toe was missing since before either of us were born, having lost it in a gambling match with a sorceress and a necromancer.

I digress.

Flipping back through the pages refreshes the memory of times my sister created havoc. This way, I can anticipate her moves and perhaps keep a step or two ahead of her. Maybe thwart her crazy-making for another decade or four.

I really was liking it in this era. I feel really whiny about leaving.

Given the combination of potions I know she's using to sort this disaster, her swans will show up tonight. I've just flipped back through to the last time we were in the same venue—Marcell and I and those blasted swans. It didn't end well for Marcell. Or rather, his tail.

Ah, well.

I really wish there was something to drink in this rectory stronger than holy water.

The Dire and the Divine

Dear Father,

I know it's been a long while since I've written. I did so enjoy our chance encounter last month at the market. You looked well, all things considered.

Mother, too.

Please let her know I harbor no ill will toward her regarding her coolness. I understand things are difficult. The consequences of my choices at the stables that night all those years ago could not have been foreseen. And even if I could go back and choose differently, I know I would not.

Tonight, though, the consequences of my choices have been laid clearly out before me. Unlike the night at the stables, I've been given opportunity—though only a few hours' worth—to think things over.

No matter what I choose tonight, my life, and therefore, regrettably, perhaps your lives, will forever be... different.

I look up from the page of horrid handwriting—being raised a stable boy didn't do the penmanship any favors. Father can read it though.

Mother wouldn't read anything I write to her. The last three letters I sent to her in Bristol were returned within the day. Her side of the family holds the longest and strongest grudges.

Part of me thinks she understands it wasn't my fault Father lost his job at Castle Rampkin. But she can't bear to know that I'm still here. With this family.

I rub my temples, hoping I don't smear ink and horse hair all over my face. I rode the fastest hackney in the whole stable to Bristol and back again in record time. I rewarded the mare with a carrot and a quick wipe-down for her assistance. I can hear her shuffling in her stall on the other side of the harness room wall.

Had I known that I'd be in Bristol again so soon, I'd have finished off this letter before and delivered it myself. One last chance to see my parents in person before the ceremony.

Before whatever happens in a couple of hours, be it dire or divine.

I shift weight from one leg to the next, trying to calm my nerves and find the words—maybe my final words—to say to them.

I rake the end of the pencil over the sandpaper, straighten the paper on the workbench, and begin again. My stomach hurts.

Of course I'll help my lord with whatever he needs. He has my loyalty. That is my choice. I will live or die by my convictions—something I admire in you both—even as I know this present predicament will most certainly drive between us an irreparable wedge.

I hope this letter will clear things up—past and present—and that in time, you'll find it in your hearts to forgive me—the past me and present one.

First, Lord Breck Rampkin holds no ill will toward you for the fire, Father. He knows that night was an accident. He knows his brother the Marquess can be near impossible if not downright ruthless in his requests, and something of this nature could've happened to the best coachmen.

To hear Lord Breck tell it, you, Father, were one of the best coachmen in all of Eldon, maybe even Bristol.

As for where the Marquess stands, you'd have to ask him. I hear him declare to Lord Breck on occasion that he's glad the horses weren't harmed. Prized animals they are.

When the Marquess speaks of this night, he often speaks of the horses. How glad he is that the stables were built back with brick and that glorious addition of a harness room. However, and I must bite my tongue, for the servant gets to have no opinion on such matters, the Marquess rarely speaks of what happened once the flames reached the steeple point. Of his brother's cries ringing out from the stable as he freed the horses from the stalls, setting them running loose.

Had I not been bringing ol' Rollins in from the back pasture, I'd have not been in the right place at the right time to assist my lord.

I pause to shudder and pace a bit. I check the lamplight. Scoot it a little more center on the bench, careful that the flame is just strong enough to see to write, and not so large to level the entire stables.

I check the cherries in the kettle I confiscated from the kitchen. I added the ingredients as instructed and now I wait.

And wait.

But I wish the process would hurry along. Maybe I made a mistake. Maybe all this sneaking around is just tearing me up and—

No. I can't go there. Lord Breck is counting on me and I want to do something special for him since this is his last—

No. I can't think that way. I mustn't. There will be time for grieving later.

Right now, this hour is the focus. The cherries. The letter. Mind the lamp.

Oh, how the night of the fire burns anew in my mind.

I pace some more and set pencil back to page.

You and Mother thought the Marquess took me on as payment for Father's sins. My father was the head coachman, after all.

But I stayed voluntarily. Because there's something you don't know, Father. You thought you'd stumbled out to the safety of the stable yard before you were overcome from the smoke. But that's not what happened.

As Lord Breck was freeing the horses, he spotted you, the flames spreading closer and closer. Taking the time to pull you out of harm's way is why Lord Breck needed saving by a scrawny stable boy.

My promotion from stable boy to footman came as a direct result of Lord Breck's insistence, or the Marquess would've replaced me otherwise. (I try to keep out of Marquess Rampkin's way, as much as possible and am oft glad when he's away on business. Come to think of it, this is the only time the Marchioness is on the castle grounds...)

If I could change things, I don't think I would. I would not decline the position or the promotion to join you and Mother in Bristol in the service of another family. I could not. He saved your life, Father. I owe him my loyalty—something I'd offer a man like Lord Breck anyway. He's a good, good soul.

I wouldn't change a thing the night of the fire, dire as it was, because all of those events lead us to tonight. You see, I'm about to watch him lay down his life for something be truly believes in—so much so that he's enlisted the help of the Dowager of Bristol.

The matchmaker.

And perhaps a witch.

I can nearly hear Mother faint dead. Father, please don't wad up the page and set it ablaze. Hear my words.

My freedom is on the line, and perhaps my life. Because after the choices and consequences were laid before me, and I had a moment to think, there was nothing to consider, really.

I will remain loyal to my lord. This is my duty. All the way to the end.

I'm writing this to give you a warning. People will talk about me. About Shedd House. About Castle Rampkin. About the Dowager. I imagine by the time you read this, Bristol will be teeming with investigators and sleuths trying to piece together thievery and magic. I wanted to warn you and there was no time to do it in person and if there were, there's no way you'd have heard me out before Mother kicked me out, so perhaps this way, you'll read the whole of the matter.

The Rampkin estate on the line with no heir, the solution the Marquess hounds on, of course, is a match and a slew of children from Lord Breck, given that the Marquess, well... We'll leave that detail to the wind.

(And to the Marchioness's adventures in France.)

But Lord Breck's soul is bigger than his mind for business. He wanted a true love match, not an arrangement for the estate's good.

So he visited the Dowager hoping for matchmaking help. More than once. The Dowager tried and failed—using human means—to pair up Lord Breck with a worthy lady. Until things hit a crescendo between the brothers, and a distraught Lord Breck ended up on the Dowager's stoop earlier today.

When he returned to Castle Rampkin, he pulled me aside and laid out my choices. And the consequences.

They are dire. But they are at the same time quite divine. A worthy quest.

∼

If I keep lifting the pencil, I'm going to fail to get this letter to Felix for delivery in the morning. I can't fail. I need to get this off my chest and...

I sigh and pull the kettle across the workbench toward me. The Dowager said I didn't need heat. Or water. Or any alcohol. Just the cherries. And the—

It's working.

On my honor, it's working!

I leap in the air and take off for the stable hall, stalls on either side. I tell uninterested mares and stallions that it worked. I stop at Ellie's stall —the mare who'd taken me to Bristol. "It worked, Ellie! Lord Breck shall have a last drink of his beloved Kirschwasser. We had no Kirschwasser, Ellie—only the cherries!"

Ellie doesn't care until I offer her a second carrot.

I nearly skip back to the harness room, the horses looking on after me as though I've lost my mind.

Perhaps I have.

I'm about to be arrested, or worse, and I don't care because I can give Lord Breck one last toast.

I need to bring along three glasses, though. That's what the Dowager said I needed to do in order to earn a tiny vial of—I don't know what, but it was yellow. It didn't even smell like brandy.

I cannot imagine who will join us in the toast. I thought it would be just myself and my lord. Surely not Lady Reniah. Or her lady's maid—who I believe I may have seen scampering down the sidewalk in Bristol as I was racing back with my vial.

My heart beats a little faster. My mind spins. Perhaps this is a silly quest, but Lord Breck would pull me aside on rare, happy occasions and we'd toast some accomplishment or another with my lord's favorite brandy.

But we had no brandy in the castle (the Marquess has been indulging of late) and the delivery due tomorrow and the ceremony tonight.

No way am I *not* bringing the third glass. Whatever the witch wants, she can have. If she can turn cherries into wine with a drop of yellow gold and mend my lord's broken heart with a drop of a different color, she can have whatever she wants.

I stand at the bench ready to finish the letter, when the realization hits me. One I've been pushing off since presented with my choices and consequences.

One consequence Lord Breck didn't articulate well.

This once-scrawny-stable-boy-turned-footman is about to lose his best friend.

I'm running out of time, Father. Time to write and time to prepare for tonight, at the very least. Events before the sun sets may lead to my demise. It may lead to you and Mother facing scrutiny. Perhaps a fast holiday elsewhere until the ruckus dies down is in order.

Contrary to what either of you think and what my actions may seem to prove otherwise, I love you both. I wish you well.

I take solace that I'll not be alone in my conundrum. Lady Reniah's lady's maid has chosen the same set of consequences, be they death or imprisonment. (How divine, really. That someone else believes the same as I—that some things are simply worth the sacrifice, society be damned... Maybe in another time, the lady's maid and I could've been matched.)

And know this: Whether I'm captured or hung, what I've done, I've done willingly on behalf of Lord Breck.

On behalf of my best friend.

And to honor the man who saved your life.

Forever your son,

Phillip

Two-Thirds of a Tale

Grimoire of William Lockridge, The Now and Again Warlock of Eldon

My sister the witch can conveniently leave out the most important details of any drama she's causing. She does this to me on purpose. How many times have I had this conversation with her?

When a magical master such as myself communes with a... magical disaster such as her, the details are important.

We must get the order of service down pat for this evening, especially since the likelihood of the townspeople catching wind and spreading word is high. Letters are no doubt being sent. Though this method is a slower means of communication than in other eras, the word is out there, floating in envelopes and tucked into servants' bags. Anything can happen.

And no matter the era, I have noticed that word spreads at a speed proportionate to the level of bad news included in said—or written—words.

And in any era, only about two-thirds of the words needed are spoken.

No one ever has the full tale.

And some of us no longer own a full tail, either.

Marcell is curled by my inkwell. His tail *almost* wrapping around his tiny body to the tip of his nose—almost.

He has my sister's black swans to thank for that. Those birds, familiars though they be, became spooked the last time my sister did a similar enchantment such as will happen this evening at Castle Rampkin. That night, they mistook Marcell's tail for the betrothed's dress adornment. Marcell was just fluffing the woman's ruffles, good assistant that he is, and the potion overreached, sparked and popped out embers, and the left swan jumped the gun and, well.

Now we have two-thirds of a tail.

And two-thirds of a tale.

And only one-third of the details we need for this evening.

I must rein my sister in, lest tonight be a three-thirds debacle.

And, unfortunately, I suppose I must do it sober.

In All The Tomorrows

I sit at the desk in my quarters after I raided my brother's stash for a piece of foolscap. It's his last sheet. Supplies are running low, the delivery from London is due tomorrow. I'll need to rise early to meet—

No, I won't.

What happens tomorrow is no longer my business.

Only what happens now.

I dip the nib in black ink and hold the quill over the paper. My hand trembles, and the next batch of Kirschwasser is on the delivery for tomorrow—

Again, with the tomorrows.

I set the quill down on the rest and stand to pace at the window. I fuss with my trousers. Purple! Some new experimental style brought back for me by my sister-in-law from France. I think the Marchioness meant this gift as a joke. What's possessed me to wear this instead of my standard black tails and pantaloons is a mystery.

Beyond the lane, I see Phillip riding into the stables. Where's he been to? Probably tying up his own loose ends, given the risk he's taking for this evening.

For me.

The pond glimmers in the late evening sun and thinking of what's to happen there in a few short hours causes my heart to pound in my chest. Nearly as it had the night of the fire. Pure energy rushed through me as the flames leapt all around. I knew I was about to die, but then I lived...

I shudder and straighten the matching purple overcoat on its hanger, I turn back to the desk. I take a few deep breaths and will the shaking to stop. I've debated on the recipient of my last words for hours. Brother or cousin? Cousin or brother?

The chair awaits. The pen is ready...

~

My Dearest Cousin Carie,

May I still call you that, or shall I lean on formalities, Your Most Eloquent Dutchess of Scottsboro?

(You can positively hear the sarcasm in my scribbles, can't you?)

I'm grinning. The first real grin I've had in a long while. Thinking back to all the childhood antics we took part in, I cannot bring myself to call you Dutchess or imagine you running your husband's estate. Or being a mother.

Bravo on that front, by the way. A legitimate heir production on the first try!

When young Theodore is old enough, you can tell him of the time his mum and Cousin Breck caught toads at the pond and set them loose in the kitchen. How the pair hid in the pantry, watching Cook lose her mind.

You can tell Theo how we snuck into the drawing room as Mr. Leads was painting Mother and Father's portrait. How we grabbed his oils when he wasn't looking—Mother and Father could do nothing but go wide-eyed, as they were sworn to stillness. How in the matter of a few moments we redecorated a section of the library wall. (The stain remains, but it's been hidden by clever positioning of a tapestry of peacocks.)

Tell him of our games of shuttlecock and skittles. Of how you cheated at Blind Man's Bluff. Of how his mum beat all her boy cousins to the point where none of us wanted you to play anymore.

Let Theo know Cousin Breck found you to be brave and caring and daring and perhaps a bit mad.

Yes, I said it. I think you're a bit mad.

You'll always be Carie to me.

And this is why I write. You're just mad enough that you may understand. And, someday, be able to talk some sense into my brother, Dutchess to Marquess.

I can no longer sit. My legs are trembling and, oh, how I long for one more drink of that cherry brandy before, well. Before I meet my true love.

I'm torn. More torn than I thought I'd be. To leave this time and go to another, even if it's on the grandest adventure I could ever imagine.

I suppose I'm a bit mad, too. Runs in the family but it affects us all differently.

Pacing across the room, around the bed I slept in for the last time last night but didn't know it. How to tell Carie this matter? I try to sort how to explain what's about to happen when I've little understanding myself.

With no time to linger, Carie, I will get to the matter.

For years, my brother has hounded and pounded on me to produce an heir—which means finding a match. Believe me, I tried. I even courted that gal your Duke suggested over in Scottsboro.

(Don't let the Duke make suggestions to anyone.)

My heart was never settled, near to breaking over the matter. Of course I care about the estate, but I want... more.

I felt like I was dead inside, but yet I lived. Day after day. Rampkin business. Travels. Entertaining. Phillip, my footman, became my most trusted confidant. His family hails from Bristol, and he told me of a matchmaker, the Dowager of Bristol. Phillip was simply telling a tale he'd heard from back home. But I thought... why not a matchmaker? Nothing else had worked.

Phillip warned me of the rumors. I know I'm hopelessly romantic, but on all other matters quite practical, so I have—had—no belief in magic.

~

The Dowager was understanding and helpful. She listened as I would drone on about expectations and pressures from the Marquess.

Things shifted in the last few months, I believe. The loneliness was intolerable to the point of despair. All the tomorrows ahead of me felt like death sentences.

Then yesterday, after a heated argument with my brother, I could take it no longer. The Marchioness has remained in France for the longest time, and my brother being frustrated beyond reason about the state of Castle Rampkin and what's to become of our line, became enraged. He threw the last bottle of Kirschwasser across the library (barely missing the peacock tapestry) and burst out of the room in a cursing thunder.

And I found myself once again on the Dowager's doorstep, distraught.

She took me in.

Gave me tea.

Listened to my woes.

And then told me she was, indeed, a witch.

Then she told me, Carie, that you *know* her. That you, my dear cousin, are a *dutchess* because of the workings of this woman.

Magical love spell or not, that's none of my business, but well done, Cousin.

Carie, the pair of us, you and me, we're quite mad, aren't we?

The Dowager gave me a vial. She gave me warnings. She give me directions. And she gave me very little time to get it all done.

This was far crazier than your rule-bending rendition of Blind Man's Bluff.

I don't know my betrothed. I've never seen this woman, though the

Dowager sent a message moments ago. I have her name. Reniah Shedd. Whether there was a bit of magic on the note I'll never know, but I was overcome with... love.

Like the kind that makes you want to live.

Regardless, I've decided to trust the Dowager in spite of the consequences to me. (Though I do regret what might happen to my footman, though he waived all concern and assisted me in carrying out the very detailed instructions.)

You trusted the Dowager once, too, and it seemed to work out for you.

You have a man you love. And I know he loves you too, you can see it when he looks at you. You have provided him an heir (and I bet more than one, given time). Your future is secure.

In all your tomorrows, your path is ordered on this earth. I am so happy for you.

In all my tomorrows, my path will forever be entwined with my betrothed beyond the veil. And I am so happy for me.

Carie, I will finally be un-alone. Grief would've claimed me in some form or fashion, rightly so and probably sooner than later. But now?

I feel alive!

I hope my words bring you some clarity. It's certainly helped me unburden.

My hand hurts now as I scribble this down. Phillip will be up soon to help me dress in this ridiculous French attire (French! I am quite mad). He'll help me ensure nothing is left undone—other than my brother's expectations.

The great Marquess Rampkin will have to tire himself out over the news before he moves forward with his life. But that's his to sort, no one else's.

Perhaps if you contact the Dowager, she can relay how this night went. I'm sure there'll be quite the commotion. I'm sure my brother will throw more than a bottle of cherry brandy against the wall. Hell. A delivery comes tomorrow, there'll be a dozen bottles to throw against a dozen walls all over the castle if he wishes to express himself in that way. (The house maids and Phillip shy away at his behavior—even old Felix cringes, and nothing phases that old goat. It's in these fits of his that I'm rather relieved the Marchioness is away so often and that the castle nursery remains unused.)

I'll ask only two things—but know that you owe this part of our family nothing.

First, if you have any clout in this parish, and if my footman, or anyone else, should be detained or arrested, perhaps you can throw that title of yours around and do a little Blind Man's Bluff rule-bending. Phillip has saved me twice, once from flames, and once with the introduction to the Dowager of Bristol.

Second, and this is the most important of all, kiss your beautiful baby son for me today.

And in all your tomorrows.

Love always,

Breck

More Than a Paper-Pusher

Grimoire of William Lockridge, The Now and Again Warlock of Eldon

Marcell and I have worked tirelessly for the last three hours securing powders from this pocket and salves from the next. That is Marcell's world, among my robes, in all the inner pockets where I keep my most prized ingredients on me at all times.

I've sewn tunnels from one pocket to the other. At any given moment, be I baptizing an infant or burying an innkeeper, Marcell travels along the fabric hollows, blending in with hues and textures and handing me this or that to make my job easier.

I do human things as humanly as possible, but it never hurts to speed things along on occasion.

Especially when one has a witch of a sister who could topple the delicate balance of Society at any given moment.

Like she has today.

Castle Rampkin may not remain upright if we have a repeat of the last time she used two vials. Jumpy swans. Missing tail bits.

Marcell and I are as ready as we'll ever be. We've armed ourselves with a balancing baste of bitters and bluebell, an equilibrium enchantment of elk horn and elderberry, and a steadiness salve of snapdragons and strawberry.

Of course my sister will *never* acknowledge all Marcell and I bring to the ceremony. It's all about her and those glorified geese.

She thinks I show up to these things just to fill out paperwork. Because I happen to be the Vicar of Eldon Parish this go-round.

I write this here in my grimoire to remind myself and Marcell and whomever may come after me as warlock, that I, William Lockridge, am more than a paper-pusher.

I am The Now and Again Warlock of wherever and whenever I might be.

But, I Digress

Once upon a time...

No, wait.

That's quite vague, is it not?

With your permission, Lord Rampkin, since time is of the essence for the lady's maid and the footman, I beg you to allow me to begin again...

The time is London's Season, but of course, you know this. I beg you once more, my lord, indulge me a moment of wistfulness as my wherewithal fades quickly and I do so love reveling in this era. One hundred years ago, things were not as they are now. And one hundred years from now, they'll be different again.

All those once upon a times.

Now is the time of sunny promenades and parasols. The time of social etiquette and escorts. Of calling cards and announcements. Of dropping hems with the modiste.

It's the time of sitting perfectly still for the artist to capture the essence of beauty on canvases and rush them to the framer. Of empire gowns and tiaras and cravats and tailcoats layered over waistcoats. It's the time of extravagant floral installments and long tables set with the most opulent bounty of the borough.

It's the time of ballrooms with spiral staircases and parquet floors. Spinning cotillions and twirling waltzes, feet light and sure.

And it's the time of hope to become betrothed in these days of dancing.

~

I sit perfectly still, as though my portrait were being painted. The nib of my black swan quill poises above the stationery while I take a moment to gather my thoughts. The late evening sun rays gleam through the inkwell, entwining with the black pigment. In a moment I'll need to light the lamp.

The spring breeze heavy with the scent of wisteria billows through the draperies and teases at my skirt hems, tickling my ankles. Fourteen windows of the gallery hall reach from the floor to the rose moldings lining the ceiling. And heaven help the housekeepers, who stand outside the hall now, no doubt bent this way and that with their ears to the door, believing their whispers to be just that. Whispers.

But I can hear them.

I lay my pen down on its rest and admire the portraits displayed around the room in the dimming light. Some on easels atop cupboards and some, taller than my lord himself, hang on all walls. The frames are crafted from the most precious materials, engraved with winding vines and ornate patterns. The canvases they embrace are of Marquess Rampkin's family. His mother, captured seated on the chaise in this very room, holding a book. His wife and two daughters. His sister in various ages—glance from one wall to the next quickly enough and you can watch her mature from a babe to a belle.

Only the portrait of my lord's brother, Lord Breck, is missing, a shadow in its place from where the same sun that's sinking now faded out the toile wallpaper around the spot the portrait once hung.

I sigh heavily.

My travel bag sits at my feet. My pairing potions are wrapped in magic and tucked tightly inside the leather pockets. Should I be taken, which hasn't happened across three centuries, the commoners will only find my shawl and writing supplies. They will not find the canvas that hung on the north wall nor its frame among my belongings.

And, heaven help them, they won't find the portrait of Lord Breck, nor that of any other soul, among the lady's maid or the footman's possessions.

It's a pity, really. The limitations of magic. My own brother is a vicar this go-round. I rub my temples at the thought. I can scarcely believe this and must remind myself of it as oft as possible, as last go-round he was a stablehand. He can cloak himself in invisibility at will and evade capture after performing his duties. It's a feat he boasts of whenever given the opportunity and of which he availed himself just last night. His limitation is in his daftness, while I have kept my wits and pairing skills but can only cloak my potions.

I sigh again and pick up my pen and dip it in the swirling ink.

A tray of sugar biscuits sits untouched. My tea has long gone cold. No matter. I must finish this earnest communique.

Lord Breck first sought me out three Seasons past as I performed my duties as a matchmaker for your Castle Rampkin. Not to boast, but my reputation proceeded me, having successfully paired dozens of matches across England, elevating ladies of lesser stations to countesses and dutchesses. Your own cousin, Lady Carie, was the recipient of my efforts, though I doubt she ever disclosed this to you.

(I assure you my potions remained lidded the entire Season when Lady Carie became the Dutchess of Scottsboro, lest you be tempted to do something idiotic to tarnish a legitimate union. You have a reputation, too, Marquess Rampkin.)

Lord Breck was heartbroken, you see. His dander up at the insistence that he hurry to marry, seeing as the lineage depended on it, given your state of, well, how to put this delicately?

Given your state of heirlessness, may the heavens have mercy on the Marchioness.

I digress.

For two Seasons I tried—and failed—to find an appropriate match in both title and taste for Lord Breck, though it was not for lack of whole-hearted effort on both our parts.

You know how these things work in the Season. A pre-planned bat of the eyelashes. An orchestrated "Oh, heavens, excuse me, your grace" and a few "pardon me, my lords." Bumps and spilled drinks and stepped-on toes.

Twirl this way.

Now that.

Come calling with flowers and sweeties and, well...

It was all to no avail. It seems love and title and the promise to continue the Rampkin lineage would die on the vine. Lord Breck did not find his soul mate in any of the ladies he'd thus far encountered. Stalwart in that endeavor, more than any man I've met across all my lifetimes. Honorable, I'd say.

Stubborn, but honorable.

(And might I add, with my lord's permission, that you tread lightly in this arena should you get the chance to live this life again—some of us do, after all, get another once upon a time, sometimes twice upon the same time. Maybe you won't need my involvement in *that* go-round should you handle such matters with a modicum of delicacy and grace.)

I digress. I'm sure you simply want to know what happened to your Breck—to the man and his portrait.

I redip my pen as the door of the hall can no longer withstand the weight of the eavesdroppers leaning from the other side. The latch gives way and four maids topple in on themselves, scrambling for footing.

The mortification on their faces is amusing, and I must stifle a smile. In its place, I send a glare fitting of my station as the rightly accused witch of a Dowager in their direction and they scramble out of the room, murmuring, "Beg pardon, your grace," and close the door loudly behind them.

The slam echoes off the hall walls.

My eyes rest on the empty spot where Breck's frame hung until last night.

Another deep breath, pen nib full of ink, and I start again.

For two Seasons, your strapping brother tried and failed to find a match. It was heart-wrenching. So much on the line. Not to mention his aching heart. He wanted a full life. To fall in love. To be loved. To thrive.

Yet this eluded him. All the pressure and formalities. Many an afternoon he'd pour his soul out to me. He wanted intimacy beyond titles and beyond the eyes thirsty for gossip in the debutante circles.

Many an afternoon, I'd see him to the door, my own spirit sinking from inhaling his hurt.

When I could bear the pain in his brown eyes no longer, I revealed my true nature to him just yesterday and gifted him a pairing potion. The purple one.

I'll forgo explaining how my methods work, my lord. I do not have the luxury of time, and neither do you, seeing how you'll need to free the lady's maid and the footman with formal apologies and get on about that heirless problem.

Or hand the estate to a cousin. Heaven knows brothers are oft pains in the asses...

But, I digress.

Lord Breck mounted his steed and galloped back to Rampkin to this great hall where I pen this letter and where you believe me to be thoroughly sequestered, which I find laughable. Lord Breck would have painted the gilded frame around his portraiture with the purple potion, just as I instructed him to. And he did it well.

I know this because in the short time it would've taken him to do the task, Reniah Shedd appeared on my doorstep.

I rest the pen in the holder once more and massage my aching joints. I stand and stare out the window over the grounds. Cricket song drifts in on the breeze, fireflies float up and away, an early dance in the dying light. I see no carriages coming up the lane that winds around the pond. I believe I'll have time to finish my story.

No.

Not my story, I remind myself. Lord Breck and Lady Reniah's story.

My story will have a very different ending than that of the young loves. And it isn't to be kept locked away here at Rampkin or anywhere else—or any time else, for that matter.

I return to my chair, smooth my skirts, and open my bag. A quick peek inside lets me know the spell holds. With all the magic I dispelled last night, I had to make sure.

Pen to paper, and I write.

Reniah Shedd was the most stunning debutante I've ever gazed upon, and I was quite shocked to see her on my step yesterday. This young lady had received a nod from the Queen herself, and even without all my matchmaking wiles—whether practical or magical—I would've bet my left big toe that she would be betrothed within a fortnight, maybe less.

She was the Season's star. Her dance card would never see an empty slot and her parlor would never not have a line of suitors, Marquesses, Dukes, Princes.

But there she stood on my doorstep. Her black hair was swept up in a simple braid around her brow, and her white day chemise clung to her delicate frame. She clutched her reticule with gloved, shaking hands.

And those eyes. Those deep sable eyes held more sorrow than I've seen across four lifetimes.

And I've seen some sorrow, my lord.

"Please, consider me for your services. I'm most certainly undone." Her lady's maid looked the other way, as though to give Lady Reniah her privacy.

Her grace nearly fell into my arms. I looked up and down the street, hoping only her maid witnessed this debacle, and brought them both inside.

I sat her exactly where your brother had been not an hour before.

"Surely, my lady, you've no need for *my* services." At this point, I still believed her to be there for practical solutions.

Not magical ones.

I thought her presence to be a coincidence, so I listened for *another* knock at my door, expecting some poor pitiful creature to show up as Lord Breck's spell-bound intended.

Because it couldn't possibly be Lady Reniah.

Lady Reniah was not a pitiful creature. The magic couldn't have worked that quickly. (But, alas, it did and I'll be sure to let my brother, the vicar, know this feat of mine.)

"I do not wish to draw this out." Lady Reniah fidgeted with her reticule. "I'm dying, Dowager."

"Oh, surely not." I blurted, then quickly regretted it as Lady Reniah gazed out the window toward the bustle of the street. She looked to be the picture of health. Pink cheeks. Good muscle tone. Bone structure fit to bear the lineage of royalty.

Her lady's maid hung her head, too, so then I knew. Lady Reniah wasted no time speaking the truth.

"I can no longer carry on as though nothing is happening. Should I divulge my secret and seek a grand title before I die? Secure the family with a fortune that my betrothed would be obligated to pay, even if I should perish on the wedding night?" She pulled out a handkerchief and dabbed her eyes. "But how can I do that to a man expecting a full life? To someone expecting an *heir*?"

And just then, I saw this beautiful soul's heart. A heart she'd gladly give to another, but not under societal pretenses. Not under obligation. But willingly and wholly, for love only.

A perfect match for Lord Breck if I ever saw one.

So I gifted her a pairing potion. The red one.

I pause to re-ink the black feather quill and light the lamp. Shadows dance off the writing desk. I take a bite of the sugar biscuit, but just a tiny one. My travels will unsettle me and it's best to go on a light stomach. I can still hear whispers and footsteps in the hall. My guards, such as they are.

❧

As stable as my magical pairing potions are, once they're opened, time is of the essence. So, I hope my lord someday forgives Lord Breck the discourtesy of not bidding you a farewell. But I pass along his heartfelt sentiment.

The couple had each been instructed by me to paint the frames of their most recent portraits with the pairing potion and meet me and my brother the vicar at the pond's edge just as the sun dipped beyond the willows last evening.

Lucky it is that Rampkin has a pond. My last magical pairing had to travel under cloak of night five boroughs away to find a suitable water source, but yours is lovely, my lord.

I digress.

I'll spare you the tedium of magical details and save me the precious minutes it would take to write them. The sun is dipping beyond your beautiful grounds once again, splaying rubies of light across the water.

I will say the potion does many things, among them making the life-size portraits light as air, and, with the help of, say, a footman and a lady's maid, Lord Breck and even Lady Reniah in her delicate state of health would have no problem at all removing the framed art from their respective walls and bringing them to the waterfront.

And, fortunate for them, the footman and the lady's maid were happy to bear official witness, having themselves borne witness over their years of faithful services to their respective employers' hearts and souls. Of the goodness that is in Lord Breck and mirrored in Lady Reniah.

I swear I'll not see the likes of their pureness again if I live in a hundred lifetimes.

The couple and their help met me at the water's edge as instructed. My brother the vicar was ready, poised with the book of rites, and though we had no time for the reading of the banns, you'll find all the appropriate paperwork in order and filed with the correct authorities.

My brother may be a pain in the ass, but he's good at this bit in spite of his daftness.

Next, my lord, I'll need you to sit, if you aren't already slumped on the chaise. You'll have a hard time believing it, no matter how well I can explain it. And, again, my time is running short. I see shadows coming across the pond. My escorts are nearly ready for me.

I write as quickly as my quill will allow and I'll try to be as clear as possible to give you some closure. And there's that matter of the footman and the lady's maid. I simply can't tolerate the thought of them locked up. Or on trial. No need, no need. And here's why...

I pull away from the desk, realizing I'd lost my posture. I put the quill down and rub my hands. I haven't attempted this much writing this quickly since that once upon a time a hundred years ago.

I endured then, and I'll endure now.

How the Marquess had me placed in this room with just the wait staff to watch over me, I cannot fathom. I suppose my age has something to do with it. I suppose I do look a bit worn out. I suppose I do look as though no one could take me too seriously. And the title of Dowager lends an air of frailty to my station. Frailty I do not possess, but one cannot account for the perception of others.

I straighten in the chair. The sun has cast its last red rays across the pond. Purple clouds hug the orb as it tries to hang on as long as possible. I smile. I think this is Breck and Reniah.

I know it is.

I pick up the quill and run the ebony barbs through my fingers. I'll need a new one soon, but no matter. My swans are coming and I'll soon meet them at the water's edge with my travel bag and shawl, wrapped in magic and ready for another once upon a time...

Are you sitting, my lord? I hope so.

At sunset of evening last, at the edge of your most magnificent pond with its topiaries and walkways hugging the rim, Reniah and her lady's maid and Lord Breck and his footman approached my pain in the ass brother the vicar, who stood ready to perform the marriage ceremony between these souls who'd never laid eyes on each other but whose hearts were already intertwined.

Your brother's tailcoat and waistcoat were of the most magnificent shade of purple. I wonder whatever possessed him to choose that hue. I'm sure if you search his wardrobe, you'll find these particular pieces missing.

His footman kept hold of his portrait through the brief ceremony.

Lady Reniah was truly a vision. Her long dark locks were piled in a dozen intricate braids and secured with scarlet and pearl combs. She wore pearl earrings and the daintiest pearl choker so as not to distract from her ballgown. No doubt the gown was stitched by the most elite modiste in all of London. Red. Layers and layers of the finest red silks made up the skirt. The bodice was bedazzled with pure white pearls. Stunning. Just stunning.

I wonder whatever possessed her to choose that hue. I'm sure, when you pass this communique along to the Shedd family, that they will indeed find these articles missing from her wardrobe.

Her lady's maid kept hold of her portrait through the brief ceremony.

My brother the vicar performed the marriage rights as the footman and the lady's maid bore witness, as my witness would be questionable at best.

You should know that Lord Breck's countenance was as bright as the noonday sun, and that Lady Reniah's eyes held no sorrow, though her hands shook in nervous anticipation, as was appropriate for the situation. Please relay this to the Shedd family. It was a happy union, if it was done in much haste.

It was at this point that I called for the portraits, and given the nature of the magic, I had no trouble lifting one giant frame in each hand and laid them out on the water of your beautiful pond. The lady's maid assisted her charge with stepping out onto the portrait, and the footman did the same with your brother.

Though wobbly at first, floating on something that shouldn't float, they each gained a steady stance on their portraits. Then the newly wedded ones danced. Feet in the frames, and arms around one another, left foot forward to the right, together. Right foot back to the left, together.

They spun and laughed, faster and faster, until purple tailcoats and red chemise blurred in the sunset. The gilded frames, their job now complete, burst into glittering powders of red and purples. The canvases soaked through likewise disintegrated and the entire pond became their dance floor.

When their most perfect waltz was over, they'd reached the middle of the pond. My black swan escorts rose from the deep and, in a most astonishing exit, escorted Lord Breck and Lady Reniah to the happy ever afterlife as husband and wife.

Having performed this particular spell many times over many eras, I'm quite accustomed to the magic by now. Nevertheless, with the sunset and the fireflies and purple and red aftereffects still glistening over the pond, it was quite breathtaking. I and my brother the vicar watched over the quiet water for the longest time, only pulling away when the wide-eyed lady's maid and the stunned footman requested that they, too, be wed that very second.

Such is the nature of my magic—sometimes the effects trickle over and one ends up with a bonus ceremony.

To this union I did bear witness, but since there's no title or estate to mess with, I hope my witness will do. My brother the vicar will have filed their paperwork, as well. He is good at this part of his duties despite his daftness, but I think I've mentioned this before. It's getting late. And I'm a bit pressed for time.

So, Lord Rampkin, this is what became of your brother and his portrait. This is what became of the sister-in-law you never had the plea-sure to acquaint. I hope, for the love of all things good, that you honor Lady Reniah and Lord Breck by caring for the Shedd estate; the couple did, in fact, wed on this side of the afterlife, and formalities are formali-ties. And somewhere in there, I'm rather confident a solution will present itself to secure the longevity of your estate as well.

Even if you pass it to your cousin.

I politely request the release of the lady's maid and the footman.

For, you now know they did not steal nor kidnap, and they are well and truly wed—the last act my brother the vicar performed before he cloaked himself in invisibility with a wicked grin and whisked himself away, leaving me and the help to be caught at the water's edge.

Brothers can be such pains in the asses.

But, I digress.

As for me, my lord, you won't know with certainty what's become of me, but this letter bears witness that you've done nothing untoward.

I'll simply begin again in another once upon a time. Perhaps we'll meet again. Perhaps you'll have learned your lesson about that modicum of grace we discussed earlier.

Alas, my wherewithal is dimming—it's the price of magic, you see. And I see across the pond that my swans have arrived. I must close now so as not to be late to the unknown era.

I do so hope one of my next go-rounds will again land in these days of dancing.

Yours Truly,

The Rightly Accused Magical Dowager of Bristol

Come Tomorrow

Eldon Parish Clergy Ledger

26 April 1818
Come this day to be wed:
Phoebe Davies of Bristol and Phillip Clarke of Eldon.
Reading of the banns waived due to special circumstances.
Stood in witness:
The Dowager of Bristol
Performed and Signed:
William Lockridge, Eldon Parish Vicar

Grimoire of William Lockridge, The Now and Again Warlock of Eldon

Come this day to be wed...

How many times have I written that in my duties as Eldon Parish Vicar? Fifty? One hundred? But these last two—in the same day and at the doing of my sister—these have worn me to a frazzle. And come tomorrow, Eldon Parish will be in an uproar.

And Bristol

And Scottsboro.

All of London, really.

But that's no business of mine any longer.

I drink the last drop of sweet cherry brandy as Marcell twitches his whiskers against my arm. He performed magnificently during the ceremony. Lady Shedd's bouquet ribbon came undone, likely due to the tremble in her hands. Marcell skittered from my pocket between my white surplice and black cassock, his fur taking on the color and texture of the garments.

He undid the bands at my neck and scampered across my arm and onto Lady Shedd's, bands trailing behind him. She handled this quite well, though Lord Breck took a step back, his footman stepping in to keep the poor man in line. With deftness of skill, the mouse retied her bouquet then retreated to my pocket where he resumed munching on his gift of cheese and bread.

Dealing with my sister the witch makes me wish I could crawl into my own pocket and eat cheese and bread.

I am humbled that my sister thought to gift me a bit of Kirschwasser—

Humbled suddenly turns to haunches rising in alarm.

Come tomorrow, what will she be up to?

I take my index finger and swipe the inside of my glass, examining the faint glow of residue on my fingertips. Marcell watches from my shoulder, looking from my finger to the empty glass, wringing his tiny hands around his two-thirds of a tail.

That nagging feeling at the back of my neck intensifies. I swear, that woman's up to something.

And come tomorrow, I'll bet my right big toe.

About the Author

Beth enjoys chucking words into sentences then standing back to see what magic—or mayhem—falls out, crafting tales in mystery, sci-fi, fantasy, and general "slice of life" fiction. She couldn't accomplish this without the help of her tutu-clad Little Miss Muse and Trudi the Concrete Office Goose, who's partial to superhero capes.

Her stories have appeared in multiple publications, including Pulphouse Fiction Magazine and Ellery Queen Mystery Magazine, and in multiple fiction anthologies. She's received several Honorable Mentions from Writers of the Future. Her lighthearted blog peeks into the writing life as she pokes fun at herself and her circus of a life.

Follow the antics of Little Miss Muse and Trudi, read Beth's blog (she might have burned down her kitchen last week), and discover the stories at bapaul.com.

Also by B. A. Paul

SHORT STORY COLLECTIONS

Spunk and Spice, Volumes 1 and 2: A Collection of six short stories celebrating timeless wit and wisdom.

Out There, Volumes 1 and 2: A Collection of six short sci-fi and speculative tales.

Mystery Minutes, Volumes 1 and 2: Six short mystery stories

All the Feels, Volumes 1, 2, and 3: Collections of inspiring short stories

Just a Tick of Whimsy, Volumes 1 and 2: Collections of fantasy shorts.

Hijacked Holidays: Definitely not your warm-and-fuzzy winter tales.

Dark Minds: Toe-curling twisted mysteries.

BLOG COMPILATIONS

Slices of the writing life with lots of laughs and bumps in the road.

Life Along the Way

Life All Over Again

NOVELS

Triage

YOUNG ADULT (OR YOUNG AT HEART) BOOKS

Switch: Book 1 in the Oliver Andrews Trilogy

Lever: Book 2 in the Oliver Andrews Trilogy (coming 2025)

Keep in Touch

BAPAUL.COM

Take a glimpse into B.A. Paul's writing journey, including the ups and downs of managing family, "real jobs," ducks in wobbling rows, and chasing down her Little Miss Muse. New blog posts go up Mondays, with the first Monday of the month reserved for a free fiction short story available on the blog for a limited time.

NEWSLETTER SIGNUP!

Get the latest release information, author updates, and exclusive content by signing up at bapaul.com.